Perfect Christmas

⊰ A Carol of Calm *in the* Midst of a Mess ⊱

by **Gary Bower**

illustrated by **Jan Bower**

KREGEL
CHILDREN'S BOOKS

Perfect Christmas: A Carol of Calm in the Midst of a Mess
© 2013 by Gary Bower & Jan Bower

Published by Kregel Publications, a division of Kregel, Inc.,
P.O. Box 2607, Grand Rapids, MI 49501.

ISBN 978-0-8254-4332-9

Printed in Mexico
13 14 15 16 17 / 5 4 3 2 1

For our grandchildren

The tree is finally standing,
but it's leaning to the right.
The twinkling lights are working,
but the star put up a fight.
Shiny things and popcorn strings
dangle from each branch.
Oh no! Careful, kitty!
You'll set off an avalanche!

But it's a perfect Christmas—
crooked tree and all—
a simply perfect Christmas,
though decorations fall.
Lord, it's still true . . .

Christmas is perfect
because of You.

*O*ur family's baking gingerbread,
which means it's time for fun!
We build a house that's sugary,
with help from everyone.
We add a smiling snowman
and some happy gummy bears.
Suddenly, the roof caves in—
time to make repairs!

But it's a perfect Christmas,
collapsing house and all.
A sweet and perfect Christmas—
Oops! There goes a wall!
But thanks to You...

Our home is strong, Lord.
Your love's the glue.

The snow is really coming down. It adds that perfect touch.
All the children dance for joy, but Daddy—not so much.
He shovels and he shovels just to make a narrow track.
He's moving very slowly now. I think he hurt his back.

But it's a perfect Christmas,
heavy snow and all.
A white and perfect Christmas—
I've never seen Dad crawl.
Please, help him heal . . .

I know You care, Lord.
Your love is real.

*I*t seems that someone's rearranged
the manger scene again.
The sheep have somehow wandered off
and joined the three wise men.
But I'll just grin and herd them back
to shepherds' watchful eyes,
and check the tiny manger bed
where baby Jesus lies.

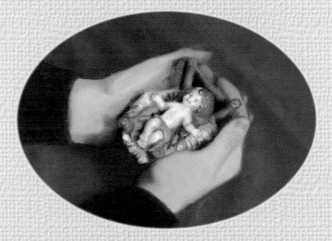

And it's a perfect Christmas—
wayward sheep and all—
a downright perfect Christmas.
Who's that in yonder stall?
We all know who...

Christmas is Christmas
because of You.

*I*t's time to gather everyone
and sing of Christmas joys.
The music we call "caroling,"
the neighbors might call "noise."
I can't remember all the words,
and someone's out of tune.
And as we sing, the neighbor's dog
starts howling at the moon.

But it's a perfect Christmas,
no matter how we sound.
A joyful, perfect Christmas.
We spread our cheer around.
And as we do…

We sing our hearts out,
O Lord, to You.

I bundle up to check the mail.
Bells jingle from the door.
No Christmas cards again? That's strange—
we sent out twenty-four.
I come inside with rosy cheeks.
There's cocoa in my mug.
Mom sits down beside me,
and says she needs a hug.

Yet, it's a perfect Christmas—
happy mail or not—
a yummy, perfect Christmas.
Yow! This cocoa's hot!
Mom's feeling blue . . .

Lord, keep our hearts warm
and close to You.

I love this special Christmas show.
Here comes my favorite scene!
Hey, what's up?! The power's out.
There's nothing on the screen.
Mom is lighting candles,
and the house seems strangely still.
Apparently we didn't pay
our last electric bill.

Still, it's a perfect Christmas,
without my favorite show—
a picture-perfect Christmas.
I love a candle's glow.
What shall we do?

In times of darkness,
we call on You.

18

This evening in our Christmas play
I had a chance to shine,
but I forgot my shepherd's staff,
and blew my only line.
Despite my disappointing night,
my parents got a lift.
Someone very generous
surprised them with a gift.

Merry Christmas!

God loves you,
and so do many people
who are praying for you.

Philippians 4:19

—Someone who cares

Oh, what a perfect Christmas!
We've been so blessed tonight
with a hope-filled, perfect Christmas.
Yes, things will be all right.
But, Lord, who knew?

Thanks for the people
who work for You.

My parents took us shopping
with the extra cash they had.
I bought a box of tea for Mom,
a pair of socks for Dad.
I'm almost finished wrapping now.
Just one more fold to go.
Uh-oh. I ran out of tape.
I'll finish with a bow.

So it's a perfect Christmas,
with gifts beneath the tree—
a fun and perfect Christmas.
Which ones are for me?
I see a few . . .

Lord, every good gift
has come from You.

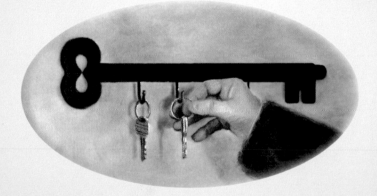

My sister snoops around the tree;
she always tries to guess.
The baby finds a candy cane—
now she's a sticky mess.
Then, suddenly poor Mom recalls
a present she forgot.
She looks at Dad—the roads are slick.
Should she go out or not?

Well, it's a perfect Christmas,
sticky mess and all.
A truly perfect Christmas.
Dad heads back to the mall,
like heroes do...

Lord, Dad reminds me
a lot of You.

23

I'm spellbound as I hear the tale
of Scrooge and Tiny Tim.
We beg for one more story,
then we sing a Christmas hymn.
And even though our bills are paid
this special, cozy night,
we still prefer to read and sing
and pray by candlelight.

Yes, it's a perfect Christmas,
with tales from way-back-when...
A cozy, perfect Christmas.
Please, read that one again!

It's fun to do
our own traditions,
dear Lord, with You.

*I*t's time to hang our stockings.
This year baby has one, too.
Hey, mine has a worn-out toe—
some candy might fall through!
But, I'll be very thankful
for whatever treats I find,
and if the younger kids get more,
I really will not mind.

'Cause it's a perfect Christmas,
and not because of stuff.
A really perfect Christmas.
My family is enough.

I guess I grew
to learn what love is
by knowing You.

The presents sure are tempting,
but I turn and head upstairs.
Morning will come soon enough,
so now I'll say my prayers.
Whatever lies beneath those bows
of silver, gold, and red,
there's only one thought on my mind
as I go off to bed:

It's been a perfect Christmas!
The very best of all!
A truly perfect Christmas!
The best I can recall!
Why is this true?
The greatest blessing
that comes from You . . .

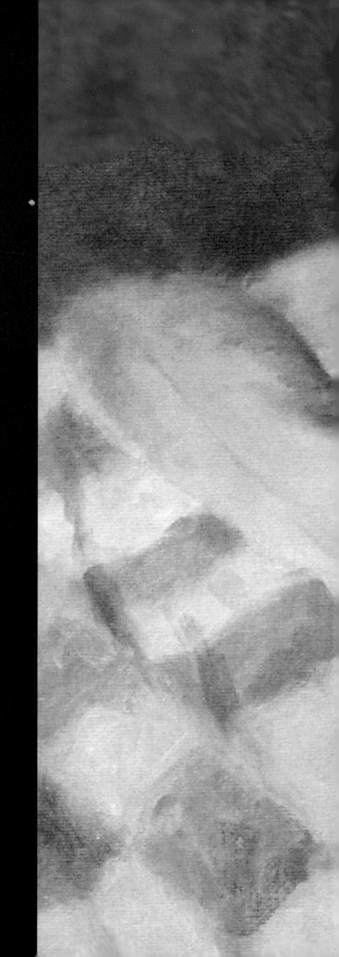

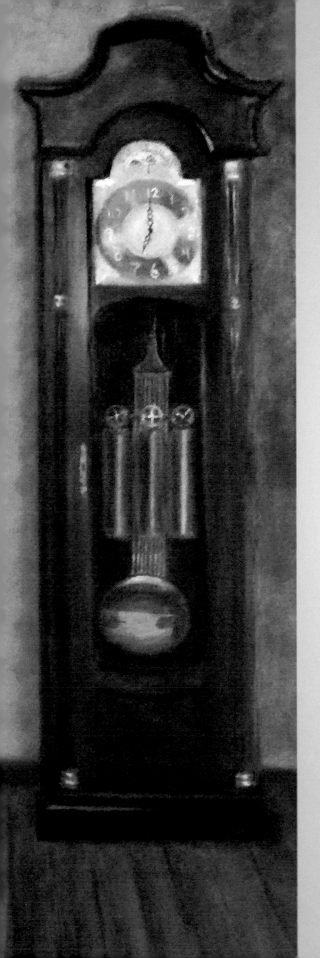

is more than...

gingerbread, gummy bears,
tippy-toeing down the stairs,
jingle bells, happy mail,
looking for a clearance sale,
wayward sheep and wise men,
shopping at the mall again,
pretty lights, caroling,
lots of howling as we sing,
old traditions, family hugs,
yummy, steaming cocoa mugs,
paying bills that we owe,
looking for the perfect bow,
snooping kids, candy canes,
heavy snow and muscle pains,
eyeing gifts that are mine,
messing up my only line,
storytime, candlelight,
hoping that the ground is white,
decorations, crooked trees...
Christmastime is more than these.
I'm convinced beyond a doubt,
a perfect Christmas is about...

Jesus

"For unto you is born this day in the city of David a Savior, which is Christ the Lord."
– Luke 2:11